The family went on holiday.
Wilf and Wilma went, too.

The hotel had burned down.

"Sorry!" said the man.

They looked at a new hotel.

"Too expensive," said Mum.

They looked at an old hotel.

"No, thank you," said Dad.

Every hotel was full.

"Sorry!" said everyone.

They had to go home.

But the car broke down.

A farmer stopped his tractor.

“Can I help?” he said.

The farmer had a bus.

"You can stay here," he said.

"What a good holiday!"
said Wilf.